LittLE Critter's®
THE Picnic
BY
MERCER MAYER

*To Jamie,
Nevis &
Alburn*

A Golden Book • New York

Western Publishing Company, Inc., Racine, Wisconsin 53404

Copyright © 1988 by Mercer Mayer. Little Critter® is a trademark of Mercer Mayer. All rights reserved. Printed in the U.S.A. No part of this book may be reproduced or copied in any form without written permission from the publisher. GOLDEN®, GOLDEN & DESIGN®, A GOLDEN BOOK®, and A GOLDEN EASY READER are trademarks of Western Publishing Company, Inc. Library of Congress Catalog Card Number: 87-83015 ISBN: 0-307-11663-8/ISBN: 0-307-60663-5 (lib. bdg.)   C D E F G H I J K L M

What a nice day
for a picnic.

Too many cars.

Too many critters.

We will find
a better spot.

This is a
good spot.

Too many cows.

I know
another spot.

What a good spot
for a picnic.

Too bad.
We have
to go.

That looks like
a good spot.

This is a
good spot.

Too many bees.

This is not
a good spot.

But this is.

Too many bears.

We can have
a picnic there.

Hello!
Is anyone
home?

Too many bats.

It is too wet
up here.

I know a
good spot.

This looks like
a good spot.

What a good spot
for a picnic!

What a nice day
for a picnic,
after all.